Ben Franklin Remembers

by Lee S. Justice

D1301776

Strategy Focus

As you read, think of **questions** about Ben Franklin's life. See if you can find the answers as you read.

HOUGHTON MIFFLIN   BOSTON

Key Vocabulary

childhood the time when you are a child

insights wise thoughts or ideas

memories things remembered from the past

original first of its kind

piece a work of literature, art, or music

present happening now; current

Word Teaser

What is a gift that's not given in the past?

The Whistle

Many years ago, there lived a boy named Benjamin Franklin. Young Ben had a pocket full of coins. The coins were a gift from a friend. Ben could spend them however he wanted. So Ben headed straight for a store that had lots of toys. On his way, he passed a boy tooting a toy whistle. Ben loved the sound of it. That's what he would buy with his coins!

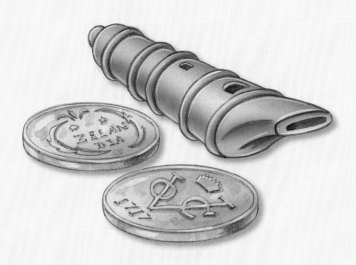

Inside the store, Ben found a whistle just like the one he had seen. He didn't even ask how much it cost. He just took the coins out of his pocket and handed them to the shop owner. Then he ran home, tooting the whistle the whole way!

Ben showed his family the whistle. When he told them what he had paid, they weren't very happy. "You spent four times what it was worth!" said his sister.

Everyone named better toys he could have bought. Their teasing upset Ben. But he knew that his family was right. He had learned his lesson. Next time he had money, he would be smarter.

Ben Franklin's Autobiography

Ben Franklin learned many more lessons as he grew up. He became a famous man. He wrote many books, and he was a great scientist and inventor. He also helped form the United States. He helped decide on the beliefs and laws that would guide our country's government.

Over the years, Ben wrote many stories about his exciting life. Some of them, such as the story of the whistle, were based on memories from his childhood. When he was an old man, he wrote a whole book about his life, called an autobiography.

A page from Franklin's autobiography

Franklin's memories made good stories. And the stories contained many wise insights. For example, the story of the whistle shows the importance of spending money wisely. It makes readers think about what they value in life. Franklin's stories also taught about things like good health, hard work, and friendship.

Franklin liked to share the lessons he learned. He decided to write an entire book of helpful advice, called *Poor Richard's Almanack*. This piece, like Franklin's other writing, was full of humor and wit.

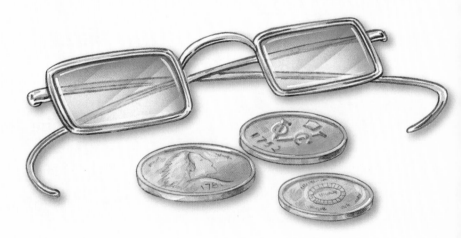

Franklin wrote his advice and lessons in short, clever sayings. They offered ideas and insights about how people could live wisely and well. Everything Franklin wrote was fresh and original, based on his own real-life experiences.

Poor Richard's Almanack became famous in both America and Europe. Ben wrote a new *Almanack* every year for 25 years.

Poor Richard, 1739.
AN
Almanack
For the Year of Christ
1739,
Being the Third after LEAP YEAR.

And makes since the Creation Years
By the Account of the Eastern *Greeks* 7247
By the Latin Church, when ☉ ent. ♈ 6938
By the Computation of *W. W.*
By the Roman Cl. 5748

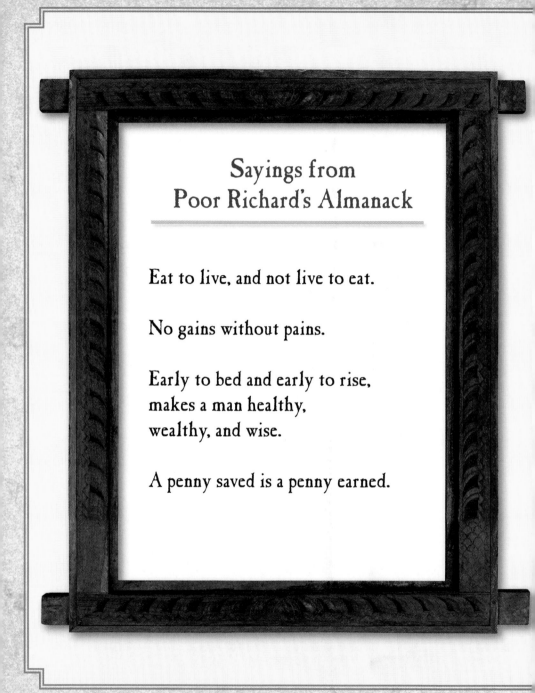

Sayings from Poor Richard's Almanack

Eat to live, and not live to eat.

No gains without pains.

Early to bed and early to rise,
makes a man healthy,
wealthy, and wise.

A penny saved is a penny earned.

Ben Franklin Remembered

Today, people still honor Benjamin Franklin. Even though the present is so different from Franklin's time, his sayings still sound true to us. They help people understand what is really important in life.

Responding

Putting Words to Work

1. Why do you think Ben Franklin's sayings still have meaning to us in the **present**?

2. Complete the following sentence:
   I'm sure that idea is not **original** because _____.

3. Use your own words to explain one of Poor Richard's **insights** quoted on page 10.

4. If you wanted to read Ben Franklin's own **memories** of his life, would you choose an autobiography or a biography? Explain your answer.

5. **PARTNER ACTIVITY:** Think of a word you learned in the text. Explain its meaning to your partner and give an example.

Answer to Word Teaser

a **present**